Joan
Aiken

Dead Man's Lane

D1136833

PENGUIN BOOKS

PENGUIN BOOKS

Published by the Penguin Group
Penguin Books Ltd, 27 Wrights Lane, London W8 5TZ, England
Penguin Books USA Inc., 375 Hudson Street, New York, New York 10014, USA
Penguin Books Australia Ltd, Ringwood, Victoria, Australia
Penguin Books Canada Ltd, 10 Alcorn Avenue, Toronto, Ontario, Canada M4V 3B2
Penguin Books (NZ) Ltd, 182–190 Wairau Road, Auckland 10, New Zealand

Penguin Books Ltd, Registered Offices: Harmondsworth, Middlesex, England

First published in *A Creepy Company* by Victor Gollancz Ltd 1993
Published in Puffin Books 1995

This collection published in Penguin Books 1996
3 5 7 9 10 8 6 4 2

Copyright © Joan Aiken Enterprises Ltd, 1993

except: *The End of Silence copyright* © 1987

All rights reserved

The moral right of the author has been asserted

Filmset in Monophoto Bembo by
Datix International Limited, Bungay, Suffolk
Made and printed in England by Clays Ltd, St Ives plc

Contents

Dead Man's Lane

IF you run hot water over the top of the whistling kettle, it lets out a howl, did you know that? I always do it when I go to my father's house, he has a whistler, and young Andy, my half-brother, he's only five, he always says, *'Don't,* Sam! Don't *do* that! You're hurting it!' Which makes me laugh.

Matter of fact, I don't go to my father's house a lot. We haven't much to say to each other. He moved last year – with my stepmother and the twins – out to this small country town, Crowbridge. It's an hour on the bike to get there. It's true he gave me the bike so that I could. And now he's promised to take me to Paris for a week, but only if I pass my exams. Which are coming up in a couple of weeks. So . . .

No problem about the exams, mind you. None that I can see. I don't know why Dad gets into such a fuss. He wrote me a letter saying he'd heard from the Old Swine that I wasn't doing as well in class as I should. Should! Who the hell is going to lay down the law about how well I should do?

Anyway, I'll be perfectly OK. Apart from anything else, I know this guy who can sell you a pen that guarantees you pass. And as well as the pen – which costs a fair slice, I will admit, but I'm going to ask Dad for an advance on my summer quarter's allowance – as well as the pen, the guy has this stuff. And the stuff is truly, truly five-dimensional. Gives you a lift right out of your own mind into something a hundred per cent higher and faster. The Great Chief Mind, maybe.

So – like I say – I don't go to Dad's place all that often any more.

When I do go, Ann, that's my stepmother, always gives me a great big hello, welcome on the mat, all that, but I reckon it can't be very sincere. Why should she be pleased to see me, anyway? I'm not hers, after all, she's got two of her own, even if one of them is a bit non-functioning. She's got no call to welcome me, and I don't trust it. If there is one thing I can't stand, it's falseness. Ann said once, 'Your father misses you. I'm glad for *his* sake.'

Well, I ask you? What can you make of that?

Last time I went to Crowbridge was a few weeks ago, to pick up some of my tapes that were still there. It's true, the kids always seem pleased enough to see me, they hug my legs; but then I reckon anybody coming to the house is a treat to them. Young Kate will always be the way she is now, she can't develop any more, there's some long medical explanation for that; Ann and my dad say it won't make any difference, she's one of the family whether she develops or not.

Easy to say that *now;* they may think differently in twenty years' time. The one it's rough on, in my view, is young Andy; he don't know what's ahead of him. Anyway – none of my business. But, for that reason, they don't have a lot of visitors coming to the house. People fight shy. You know.

Well, I went down to pick up my tapes. The way you get to Dad's place in Ferry Road, Crowbridge, there's a really crafty short cut. Gives me a terrific feeling every time I use it.

As you get to the town, the main road from 3

Galhampton turns left at the bridge, and then you have to circle right round Crowbridge on the perimeter road, across a pair of roundabouts, and then back into Warden Street. It's all a one-way system.

Whereas, if you take the cut down Dead Man's Lane, you are there in a brace of shakes.

It was Ann who first showed me the short cut; she's lived in the town before, see, and knows all its crannies like the palm of her hand. As you come down the hill, Pelican Hill, it's called, named from the pub up at the top, you have to watch out very, very sharply, because it's a little, inconspicuous turn, looks more like somebody's private driveway than a public road. And in fact there are two private driveways before you come to it, so you have to watch for the third entry, which is Dead Man's Lane. Why it's called Dead Man's Lane I don't know, and Ann doesn't know either. Some dead man long, long ago. Whatever he did, or what happened to him, must have been pretty impressive, for the lane to be called after him. It's queer that nobody seems to remember.

4 The lane isn't at all long, maybe a quarter of a mile,

and halfway along there's an acute left-hand bend. Lord help you if you meet somebody coming the other way, for – would you believe it – they've never made Dead Man's Lane into a one-way road, I suppose because so very few people actually know and use it. At the bottom end it turns into Rope Walk, and *that* leads into Warden Street, where you only have to turn right and there you are in Ferry Road. Saves all that circuit round the town.

But the thing is, you have to be really nippy, coming down Pelican Hill, to judge your moment and slip across in front of the opposing traffic, into that tiny little deep-cut entrance. It always gives me a terrific zing when I do it on the bike – one minute you are chugging down the main road, among the heavy traffic, buses, trucks going to the harbour, hundreds of tourist cars, then – zwoosh! – you are out of it all, zipping down between those high narrow banks, with close-packed trees and bushes making a tunnel of it, thick and dark, arching over your head. Round the sharp left-hand bend, holding your breath in case there's something on the other side coming towards you – which, up to now, there never *has* been – and then, like coming out of a tube, you are back in bright daylight, rolling into Rope Walk, which has little red-brick Victorian cottages on one side, with box-sized front gardens. On the other side there's old timbered storehouses and a car park. The whole trip along Dead Man's Lane takes only a couple of minutes – less, maybe – but there's a kind of nippy thrill about it – like surfing, or swallowing an oyster, or the Big Wheel.

I lie awake at night, sometimes, thinking about it. Funny, though – it's not *possible* to lie awake thinking about it for more than a moment or two: it always puts you to sleep. Better than counting sheep! The one really sure-fire soporific; it works every, every time. I've sometimes thought it should be possible to patent it, to those guys who do operations without anaesthesia, by hypnotising their patients; you get an awkward one who won't respond to hypnosis, you just take him down Dead Man's Lane a couple of times and then get him to go into recall. Of course he'd have to be able to ride a bike, that's one problem.

Well, the last time I went to Dad's house was a bit of a frost. Why, I still am not quite sure. I got there, Dad wasn't in yet, he took some dreary job, teaching at the local Middle School. Had to get what he could, as they wanted to live in the town. And he was off organising a botanical excursion, wouldn't be in for a couple of hours, though it was a Saturday.

I'm never going to get married. I just don't see all this adapting your life-style and habits to suit another person, because they want to live in a place. I'm going to set myself up in one room with all my electronic equipment – as soon as I'm able – and that will be that. Then I'll do what I want.

Anyway, I walked into the house in Ferry Road and the twins each came and grabbed a leg; then, after a while, Kate crawled off, in her dopey way, but Andy followed me wherever I went. He can talk the hind leg off a mackerel, that one.

I was hunting for my tapes, and, of course, they'd all been *put away*. I had a hideous job finding them, had to shift half the furniture in the downstairs rooms to get at them in the cupboards where they had been stowed. There's a million cupboards in that house – I reckon that's why Ann likes it so, she's got what I'd call an obsessionally tidy nature, she can't stand to see things lying about in the open; when the kids have finished playing, every block has to go back into its box, trucks into their garage, crayons into the tin, paint water emptied, paper stacked together – it's enough to give the kids hang-ups that'll last into their nineties, if you ask *me*. Which nobody does. Of course maybe when you are in your nineties you prefer to have the ballpoints all sorted into their separate colours. I wouldn't know.

Anyway Andy helped me shift the big couch, and the chests and other things so as to get at my tapes – he loved that, he thought it was a great game to drag all the furniture into different places. And I made a heap of the tapes, for Dad had said he'd put the bike on the car roof-rack and drive me back that night.

Ann had gone off round the corner to the little GoodBuy Supermarket which is all they have there, she said it was a good chance for her to go out while I was there to babysit, and she'd get her hair done at the same time.

Luckily Kate had fallen into one of her endless naps, I'd really hate to have to be responsible for *her*. Andy's no problem, I'll say that for him. He just chats along.

When I'd got the tapes sorted out I was hungry – hadn't had any breakfast before I started out from Mum's – so I went and took a look in the fridge. Got out some pizzas and some chops and some other things that were there, and stuck them in the micro-wave. And ate the lot. Plus a big tub of buttercandy ice-cream, and a cake and some ginger buns that I found in the pantry. Moving all that furniture about had really hollowed me out. I asked Andy if he wanted any, but he said no, they'd only just had their lunch when I got there. At two o'clock! I ask you!

Then I remembered I wanted to make some shelves for my bedroom back at Mum's, so I went into Dad's workshop and found a couple of boards, and brought them into the kitchen, where it was warmer – I don't know how Dad can stand that cold workroom of his – and sawed them up. Andy loved watching that. He wanted to try sawing, but of course I 9 wouldn't let him. But I let him play with the sawdust. He made it into patterns on the carpet.

While I worked, I was telling him about coming down Dead Man's Lane.

'*I* know Dead Man's Lane,' says Andy, 'we go that way when Mum takes us to the Bluebell Woods. Up Dead Man's Lane, up Pelican Hill. At my school they sing a song about Dead Man's Lane.'

Andy goes to school though he's only five. Kate doesn't, of course, and never will. But I reckon Ann is glad to get one of them off her hands for a few hours.

'What's the song?' I say to Andy, thinking maybe it'll explain the name.

He sings:

'Dead Man, Dead Man, in Dead Man's Lane,
Tell me once, tell me again,
Tell me all I want to know,
I'll be your friend if you do so.
Three times, three times round
Drive three times round the town

> Then down Dead Man's Lane you go
>
> And he'll tell you all you want to know.'

The tune, sung in Andy's droning little voice, was a bit like Baa Baa Black Sheep. I get him to sing it again, then I join in, and we have a real good time. Kate never wakes.

In the middle, Dad comes back. I suppose by now it's about half past five. He seems a bit annoyed — what about I can't make out — and then Ann comes back, and he lights into her because tea isn't ready. Ann's your silent sort, she never says anything, just puts on a kettle — it boils right away, and screams like a banshee because I'd had it on, just before, to make a big jug of coffee and choc mixed.

'I'll just go out for a few things,' Ann tells Dad, looking rattled, and out she goes again. Dad stumps about — spreading sawdust everywhere — and says nothing either.

So I listen to a few of my tapes till Ann gets back, and then Dad says, 'While she's making a meal, I'll take you back.' That surprises me, as I thought I was to spend the evening there, but, OK, I collect my stuff and take it out to the Escort.

Kate's still asleep, but I say goodbye to Andy – Ann's in the kitchen frying chops, she gives me a kind of wave with her face turned away over the cooker – and then we slam off in Dad's car with my bike on the roof. And he gives me this long saga about working harder at school.

I don't listen to him much because I know perfectly well that I'm going to be all right. I'm absolutely sure of that. I do remember, though, to get the extra quarter's allowance out of him, though he's pretty glum and surly about it.

'What do you want it for?'

I owe a couple of the fellows, I tell him, and he's glum about that too.

'And when you do come down here – I wish you'd be more considerate to Ann –'

That really knocks me. 'What did I do wrong, for Sam's sake?'

He just shrugs. And I begin to think the trip to Paris is off. But no, he still refers to it. Only if I pass the exams. And he wants me to come down to Crowbridge the week before. 'That way,' he says, 'you can get some revision done in peace without all those friends of yours hanging around.'

Well, OK; I don't argue. By then I'll have got the special pen — warranted to work, never fails — and some more of the stuff, the powder. Power powder, they call it. You sniff it — a little, but not too much, specially before a bike ride. Never too much.

So I say goodbye to Dad, and he drives off at top speed, as soon as I have my things out of the car, because he's always dead scared of running into Mum.

He seems a bit sad. I never know what he's thinking.

And that night, when I go to bed, I remember Andy's little rhyme: 'Dead Man, Dead Man, in Dead Man's Lane . . . ' and I say it over and I'm off to sleep as quick as blowing out a match.

So now it's the week before the exams, and I'm on my way back to Crowbridge. A dull, rainy afternoon.   13

And, as I come to the top of Pelican Hill, I remember the rhyme again. 'Three times, three times round, Drive three times round the town . . .'

Just for laughs, I think, I'll *do* that. Three times round the circuit of the perimeter road – it'll be a game to see how fast I can get around Crowbridge, I'll check the speed on my digital radio – up the hill again, round the roundabout at the top, then, zing! back down the hill, and into Dead Man's Lane.

So that's what I do.

First circuit takes four-and-a-half minutes; by the second I've cut it to four. Third in slightly under four, I'm really getting the feel of it now. Up the hill in a rainy streak, round by the old Pelican pub – then down again, with the air cutting away from me in bow-waves that you can almost *see*.

Across in front of the traffic – there's some braking and skidding, but not from *my* front wheel, which clips neatly in between the high entrance-banks of Dead Man's Lane – and now we're hurtling, we're zooming down the green tunnel, through the smell of wet green leaves and mud.

And now we come to the left-hand bend – and round beyond it I believe the Dead Man is waiting, waiting to tell me all I want to know. . .

The End of Silence

IT was after Ma died that our father acquired the owl, and we started to hate him.

She was killed by a bomb. It happened at Frankfurt airport, when she was on her way back from a visit to Aunt Ginnie. 'Goodbye, see you next Saturday, I've left enough cooked food in the freezer for a week, and I'll try to bring back some German rock records,' she had said, when she left, six days earlier, and that was the last time we saw her. Death is extremely shattering when it comes baldly and unexpectedly like that; if somebody is ill, or in hospital, you have a little time to adjust, a little time for your mind to prepare. But in such a situation as ours, no way. I know this sounds obvious, but when you yourself are the victim, the truth of it really hits you.

We were all knocked out in different ways. My sister Helen went silent. I began addictively eating tortilla chips and reading murder mysteries. Bag after bag of chips, book after book, two or three a day. I got them from the local library or bought secondhand paperbacks from the Old Bus Station Wholesale Goods Mart. 'You'll get horribly fat if you don't stop,' Helen broke her silence to say. But I couldn't stop. Reading was a drug that numbed the pain.

Father came out worst. He went silent too, and lost a couple of stone in weight. Then he suddenly announced that he was sending us to boarding school.

His explanation *sounded* reasonable.

'I'm a writer, damn it! I've got to support us all and keep up the mortgage payments. My inventive faculty has to keep functioning, which is hard enough in present circumstances, Lord knows. How do you think I'd manage if I had to keep remembering about things like fetching you from school and stew for dinner?'

Ma would have managed somehow, if she'd been the one who was left, I thought but didn't say. Helen pressed her lips together and stared at her feet and then turned and walked away.

Apart from the shock of losing all our friends and familiar surroundings at one sweep, the boarding 17 school wasn't too bad. People knew what had happened to us and were kind without making a fuss. Our connection with Father was a help, I suppose. He is fairly well known because, besides being a poet and an expert on Anglo-Saxon, he wrote that book about Alfred and the Danes, *The King's Jewel,* which they did on television and it was very successful.

Which was one reason why we took his excuses for packing us off to boarding school with more than a pinch of salt.

'He just wants to get rid of us,' I said, 'because we remind him of Ma.'

'Well – he does have to look ahead,' Helen argued. 'One TV success won't last for ever. And it's four years since he wrote the *Jewel.* I'm sure he isn't doing any work. He just goes into the study and sits. I've seen him, through the window.'

'That's why he doesn't want us at home. He's afraid we'll ask what he's working on.'

When we went home for Christmas, there was the owl.

Aunt Joe had given it to Father. She's a vet, and

someone had brought it into her surgery with a hurt wing, probably done by a car. 'Your father needs something to look after,' she told us. We would rather it had been us.

Walt Whitman was the name Aunt Joe had given the owl. It was a big bird, a pale barn owl, about a foot high, large as a cat, with a fawn-coloured back and skull feathers ending in a sort of Venus peak over its eyes. The rest of its feathers, front, face, and under-wings, were snowy white. The eyes were huge, black, and staring. I suppose it was a handsome beast, really, but we hated it. We felt it had supplanted us. There was something spooky and startling about its habits – you never knew where you would come across it suddenly, in the airing cupboard, or staring at you from the top of a bookshelf, or the handlebars of Helen's bike, or the kitchen dresser, or the oven. The oven and the medicine cupboard were two of its favourite spots.

'It's not hygienic!' Helen stormed at Father, but he said, 'Rubbish. Owls are very clean creatures. And Whitman has completely cleared this house of mice. There isn't one in the place nowadays.'

That was true. Mice had been a problem before. You do get them in old houses.

Whitman spent a lot of time in Father's study, perched on top of a bust of the poet Edgar Allan Poe. And because of this, Father insisted that we always knocked before going into the study – 'So as not to startle Whitman.'

'Really I bet it's to give Father time to look as if he's been working,' Helen muttered.

But Father insisted that the owl *helped* him to work; its soundless presence in the room was an aid to concentration, he explained. I remembered that he used to say the same thing of Ma. 'The only person in the world whose being in the room didn't prevent me from thinking,' he had said about her, and sometimes he called her 'My gracious Silence'.

The owl affected our life in a good many ways. The landing window had to stay wide open at all times, rain or fine, hot or cold (and at Christmas it was *very* cold) for Whitman's comings and goings. The TV had to be turned off at ten sharp because, Father said, Whitman didn't care for the noise and

20

vibration. Our friends with dogs were severely discouraged from coming to the house; in fact our friends were discouraged altogether; Whitman, said Father, didn't care for a lot of laughter and voices, or thumps and pop music, or smells of sausages and chips cooking. Whitman didn't like Helen practising the cello, according to Father, and he simply hated the sound of my trumpet.

'That bloody owl's just an excuse not to have us in the house at all!' Helen burst out one evening, close to furious tears because Father wouldn't let us give a party.

'Helen! I will not be spoken to like that! In any case I don't know how you can have the heart even to think of giving a party so soon after Marian –' His voice dried up and he sat staring at Helen with what seemed like hate.

'Don't you see, you silly man, it's because we want to take our minds *off*? How can we do that, when we have to tiptoe about all the time as if the place was an – an Intensive Care Unit?' And then Helen rushed out of the kitchen and up to her room, slamming doors all the way. 21

And Whitman, disturbed, left his perch on the plate rack and ghosted about the house on great pale wings, as if blown by an invisible gale.

Father simply stared at the calendar, obviously willing the last week of the holidays to go by at double-quick speed.

When we came home at Easter it was the same, only worse. Whitman was plainly fixed with us for life. Father had formed the habit of buying him little delicacies at a pet shop: foreign mice and lizards, things like that. The owl was more relaxed in our house; he made more noise than he had at Christmas, suddenly let out a weird shriek every now and then, which could startle you almost out of your wits. Or he would do a kind of loud snore, also very disconcerting, or suddenly snap his beak together with a loud click. He was not a restful house-mate. Despite this increase in vocal activity Father had, to our discomfort, begun to address the owl as Silence. Whitman, he said, was a silly name, not suitable, not dignified. Besides, Whitman was a silly poet. Silence was much more suitable.

All the old rules and regulations were in force, and some new ones too. Transistors were totally banned, so was playing table tennis. Father was afraid that Silence might get over-excited and swallow one of the balls, which could kill him.

'I wish it would,' said Helen furiously. 'If Father were to *marry* again, I suppose I'd hate it, but at least it would be possible to understand, and sympathise, because he's lonely and — and unfulfilled; at least that would be *natural*. But to be tyrannised over by a beastly *owl* — that's just absolutely *un*natural and spooky — it's like something out of those Poe tales that Father used to read us.'

In the old days, when Ma was alive, we all used to read aloud to each other quite a lot; now we never did any more. I daresay, if pressed, Father would have been able to come up with some reason why Whitman — Silence — wouldn't like it.

'Do you think we could kidnap Whitman?' I suggested. 'Pick a time when Father's out of the house, put the beast in a basket, and take him off on our bikes to some distant spot, and leave him there?'

'We could try,' said Helen.

So we tried. We rode twenty miles – to Cranfield Forest – and left Whitman on an oak stump.

He was home before we were. So that was no good.

'Owls are very place-oriented,' Helen said. She had been reading about them in the bird book. 'They use the same nest year after year. Obviously Whitman looks on this house as his nest now . . .'

'Well then I think we have to murder him.'

'*Murder* him!' Helen looked aghast; but then she looked thoughtful.

For days we went around without speaking; we were all of us obsessed by the owl, one way or another. The awful thing was that he did, in some way, remind me of Ma; there was something about his pale face and widow's-peak brown cap and great dark eyes that somehow called up her face, but in a teasing, horrible, unreal way. I suppose that may have been at the bottom of his fascination for Father.

I spent hours racking my brain to think of some 24 foolproof way to get rid of the owl. It would have to be done without the least chance of arousing Father's suspicion, or the results would be dreadful: he'd probably kick us back to school and forbid our coming home at all, send us to labour camps in the holidays and never speak to us again. But really, for his welfare as much as ours, I thought the deed must be done, only how? Poison, for instance, was out of the question; anything of that kind would point to us.

One night, after thrashing about wide awake for hours, I got up long before dawn. I sat hunched on my wide window-sill, gazing out. Our house lay on the edge of the town and beyond our garden hedge was a big hundred-acre field of young winter wheat, beginning to grow thick and green; beyond that lay a little wood. The sun, on the right, came up into a dim red cloudy sky like a thin melon-slice of blazing gold; into this theatrical light came a buoyant flitting shape which I soon recognised as Whitman, methodically quartering the wheat-field for breakfast. He flew quite silently, coasting with very little effort; then, sometimes, suddenly dropped with a wild flapping of wings. I've read that a barn owl can bring 25 back a mouse to the nest every fifteen minutes. I don't think Whitman caught as many as that; but then he had no chicks to feed. The situation was unnatural for him too. Seen flying, his body looked wedge-shaped, and the wide pale wings looked almost translucent with the marmalade-coloured sunlight coming through them. And then, Mother's face looking out between them, when he turned his big black eyes in my direction . . . He has *got* to go, I thought, though at that moment I felt quite sad about it; he was so handsome, coasting to and fro in the early light that, just then, I felt a kind of sympathy with Father. All the same, he has to go, or we shall end up stark crazy.

It was at that moment I had the idea how to do it.

Father was due to go up to Edinburgh that day, to receive an honorary degree from the university. No cash in it, just bags of honour, he said rather drily. Still, it would be beneficial for him to get away, the first time he had done so since Ma's death, and he would stay a night in Edinburgh and return the following day.

He gave us endless instructions.

'Don't forget to lock up, last thing. And make sure all the lights are out. And mind you leave the landing window open, so that Silence can fly in and out.'

At least we didn't have to worry about feeding Silence; he was a pet who provided his own diet, to do him justice. Though I didn't doubt Father would bring him back some fancy tit bit from Scotland, Celtic mice or Caledonian lizards. Whitman's presents at Christmas had far outnumbered ours, which consisted of an obviously last-minute chemistry set and paintbox.

Father left only just in time because road-works were in progress along our stretch of lane: a new water main was being laid, there were men with drills and a great excavator and a stretch of muddy trench on one side of the road, and a long lumpy ridge where the completed ditch had been filled in. The sound of the digger and the pneumatic drills had been steadily coming closer for the past three days; Whitman hated it, and so did Father; he was really delighted to get away to Edinburgh, and particularly 27 today, when the work would be right outside our house. In fact if he had delayed his departure by another ten minutes the men would have dug their trench right across our garage entrance and he would have had to make his journey by bus and train.

We never kissed each other for greetings or farewells any more. 'Behave yourselves,' Father called, flapping his hand out of the car window, and then he drove away quickly, under the snout of the digger, which was just getting itself into position.

'Where's Whitman?' I said to Helen, as we put away the breakfast dishes.

'In the pantry. Why?'

'I've had the perfect idea. Come on: we'll do it now, and then we'll go out for the day. Take a picnic to Bardley Down. The house is going to be unbearable all day, anyway, with that row outside.'

We found Whitman dozing on the pantry top shelf. He did that most of the day, sometimes snoring, as I have said.

By now he was quite used to us, and only snarled and grunted a bit as I picked him up and sat him in the gas oven, on the lowest rack, having taken out the others. Then I shut the door and turned on the gas.

After that, feeling like murderers — as we were — we grabbed some cheese and apples, locked front and back doors, and fled from the place.

'There won't be any sign of how he died,' I said. 'Father can't possibly guess. He'll probably think Whitman died of old age. After all, we have no idea how old he is.'

'Father will be horribly upset,' Helen said wretchedly.

'Maybe that will be good for him.'

'Just so long as he doesn't go and get another owl . . .'

We had a ghastly day. It was cold and cloudy, not quite raining, but raw; we had brought along books in our packs, but it was too cold to stop and read them, so we walked and walked, in a huge circle, and ate our lunch standing, in a big yew forest where the trees gave us a bit of shelter, leaning against one of the big reddish trunks. At one point we heard the unmistakable screech of an owl – 'Yik, yik!' in the gloom.

'Whitman would have liked it here,' Helen said sadly.

'It's no use, Nell. You know he'd only have come boomeranging back. We did try . . .'

At last, more dead than alive, we limped home ourselves, just as dusk was beginning to fall.

We had planned what to do: open doors and windows to let the gas escape, then retreat to the greenhouse for twenty minutes. The greenhouse was kept at an even temperature by an oil heater; it was the first time we had been warm all day.

'The gas ought to have dispersed by now,' I said finally.

So we went cautiously indoors and flung open lots more windows. I turned off the gas and opened the oven door just a crack. I didn't look inside the oven. Hadn't the heart. Thought I'd wait till morning.

'I'm going up to bed,' I said. 'Don't feel like supper.'

'Me too. Is it safe to go to sleep, though?'

'Open your bedroom window wide. And don't go striking any matches.'

We crept to bed. I had expected to lie awake, racked by guilt and horror at the deed we had done. But I didn't; I slept as if I had been karate-chopped.

It was Helen who lay awake. When she came down in the morning I was alarmed: she was whiter than Whitman's shirt-front.

'Ned! *Whitman has been haunting me all night!*' she croaked. 'He's been perched on my bed-rail.'

'Oh, come on!' I said. But I was pretty scared myself – not of ghosts; I thought Helen was having some kind of breakdown. She looked so white and wild and trembling that I wondered if I ought to call the doctor.

'He made me think of Mother!' Helen wept. 'Oh, Ned – why in the world did we do it?'

Just then Whitman – or his ghost – came coasting into the room on silent wings.

'Keep him away – keep him off me!' Helen shrieked.

Whitman made for the oven – the door of which

stood open. And that made me realise for the first time that there was *no corpse inside.*

'It's all right, you dope – he's *not dead.*'

At that moment there came a peal at the front door.

'Gas inspector,' said the man who stood there. 'I've come to reconnect you and check.'

'Reconnect –?'

'Didn't you know? The excavator cut the gas main yesterday. All this row of houses were cut off. Hey, what the blooming –?'

He had suddenly come face to face with Whitman, sitting in the oven.

'Oh, that's our owl,' I said, weak and idiotic with relief. 'He, he likes sitting there.'

'Pretty stupid, dangerous place to let him sit,' said the gas man. 'Unless you fancy roast owl.'

And he went about his business of reconnecting and testing.

That day we stayed at home. Our spirit was broken. We endured the hideous row made by the excavator and the drills – a few yards farther along, now; we

32

did our school holiday work and washed some clothes; I mowed the lawn, Helen made a shepherd's pie against Father's return. That meant turning Whitman out of the oven. Restless and displeased, he found himself a new perch on the front hall coat-rack. I suppose being shut inside the oven had insulated him nicely, the day before, from the noise of the drills and the thuds of the digger.

'I hope they don't cut the gas main again,' said Helen. 'I'm dying for a bath.'

At tea time, Father came home. Cross and tired, he flung open the front door – and Whitman flew out, straight into the jaws of the excavator. One crunch, and he was done for . . .

Father and Helen wept in one another's arms.

'He was so like Mother,' she sobbed. 'He had just her way of looking at you and not saying anything –'

'Yes, yes, I know, I know –'

Father didn't blame us. How could he? The death of Silence was nobody's fault.

But of course we feel just as guilty as if we had really murdered him. After all, we meant to; it was pure chance that our intentions came to nothing. We really are murderers.

Helen seems to have washed away her guilt in tears, and in looking after Father. But I haven't: I suppose because the gas oven was my idea. And I suppose it is because of that guilt that Whitman haunts me and not Helen.

Night after night, there he is, perched on my bed-rail, silent, motionless, staring at me with Mother's eyes. Whether I'm at school or at home, it makes no difference. Nobody else sees him.

Strangely enough, I'm starting to grow rather fond of him.

Toomie

WHEN you travel with a ghost, your problems can be really acute.

Julia and I had hoped, of course, to get off to France without Toomie. But our hope was not even founded upon sand; it was founded on thin air.

As soon as plans for the summer holidays at Ste Baume leaked out, the demands began.

'Can we bring Toomie with us? Please – oh *please!*'

'We *can't* leave poor Toomie back at home. All on his own! That would be wicked!'

'She'd be so lonely!'

For a long time, it had been thought that Toomie was a boy.

'He wears boys' clothes,' said Marianne.

'But that's because it's safer. He's really a girl. He told me so *himself,*' argued Tom, who was two years younger.

'Why was it safer?'

'Because – because – people might hurt him,' said

Marianne. 'His father used to beat and bang him *dreadfully*.'

'But his own father must have known whether Toomie was a boy or a girl?'

'It wasn't really his father – it was only his – his – stepfather.'

Large areas of Toomie's life remained pretty vague. Julia and I felt this was just as well, for it had plainly been a short and unhappy one. Nor were we able to discover precisely when he had lived.

Tom said: 'He's still alive *now*.'

'No, silly, that's only his ghost,' said Marianne. She frowned in thought. 'When Toomie was here it was a very long time ago. In the war.'

She could not tell which war.

'When there wasn't much food.'

That might have been any war.

'We've told her about France. We've told him how lovely it is at Ste Baume. He really, really wants to come.'

'She's never been in any other country but
36 England.'

Privately, Julia and I hoped that, when it came to the point, Toomie would be unable to leave Camberwell. Surely ghosts don't usually go abroad? But the drive to the airport showed that, so far, the migration presented no problem.

'You can sit between us, Toomie. But you can sit up on top of Tom's pack, so you'll be able to see out. Look, look at all the buses.'

And, at the end of the flight, the lady who had shared their three-seat row in the plane said to Julia nervously, 'It's really wonderful what imagination children have nowadays, isn't it? I suppose they learn to play these games at school?' before making off hastily into the airport with her hand luggage.

At the Lyons airport our trouble started.

Toomie, it seemed, was fascinated by the luggage carousel. As is always the way, our five large duffel bags were the very last to be extracted from the plane's hold, and in the meantime we had spent half an hour watching other people's wooden boxes, rolled-up mattresses, easels, outsize pink teddy bears, infra-red grills, and plaster peacocks whirling round and round on the conveyor belt, unclaimed, and apparently unrequired by their owners. The things that people take with them on their travels! But few of them, I thought, as unwelcome or as inconvenient as Toomie, who, according to Tom and Marianne, now hopped on to the belt, between the pink nylon ted and the infra-red grill, and was borne off through the flapping rubber fringe.

'Oh, TOOMIE! Come back!'

'What's the matter, Marianne?'

'Toomie's gone off with the luggage!'

'Don't worry, he'll come back in the other way,' said Tom robustly. 'Yes, look, there he comes. Oh Dad – can *I* do that too? Can I get on the luggage belt?'

'No, you certainly may not.'

'But Toomie did.'

'Toomie's a ghost. We aren't responsible for what he does. But you'd better tell him to get off. Any minute now our luggage will come through, and then we're leaving. Yes, look, there is one of the bags.'

By the time all our bags had turned up, Toomie, it seemed, had fortunately had enough of riding the carousel and was prepared to accompany us to the car rental counter, where a great many forms had to be filled in. The children grew restless and impatient.

'Toomie doesn't like it here.'

'Well, he'll have to put up with it, like the rest of us,' Julia said shortly. 'Do you want to go to the loo? Down those stairs.'

Toomie, it seemed, was immune to such needs. One advantage of being a ghost. But when the children came back, they fell into panic and anguish.

'*Where's Toomie?*'

'I don't know,' said Julia crossly. 'Isn't she here?'

'No.'

'No!'

'Toomie! TOOMIE! *Where are you?*'

At this moment the rental formalities were completed.

'Come on,' I said. 'Our car is in the car park, at the very farthest end. As usual. Everybody please carry one piece of luggage.'

'We've got to wait for Toomie!'

'We certainly have not. If that ghost chooses to wander off that's entirely his own concern. We have a four-hour drive ahead of us, I'm not waiting any longer or we shan't get there before dark. Come on!'

With Tom in tears and Marianne biting her lip, we humped our bags and struggled across the car park. Even Julia seemed concerned.

'Look –' she said. 'I know it's all just – But if we start the holiday in such – I mean, it's going to be hard to – Well, I don't know exactly how we –'

Luckily, as we were ramming the last of our enormous bags into the tiny luggage compartment of the hired car, the problem solved itself.

'Oh, TOOMIE!'

'Where *were* you all this time?'

'We thought we'd *lost* you!'

'Will you please tell that ghost not to wander off any more,' I snapped, as Julia stuffed the children into the back with drinks, biscuits, comics, books, and listening apparatus.

40   'He thought he saw Chap,' Tom explained, as we

threaded our way out of the airport complex and took the road south. 'He hasn't seen Chap since he died. Chap, I mean. He's always looking for Chap.'

'And who, pray, is Chap?'

There was a moment's silence while explanations were imparted.

'Chap was Toomie's dog. But he was killed. It was very sad.'

'Something perfectly dreadful happened to Chap.'

'What kind of dog was he?' Julia hurriedly asked, hoping to bypass any account of Chap's dreadful end.

'One of those dogs with flat, squashed-up faces.'

'A bulldog? A Boston terrier?'

These terms, apparently, meant nothing to Toomie.

'He was brown.'

'And quite big.'

'Anyway,' said Julia, 'if Toomie is a ghost, and Chap is a ghost too, why can't they – well – get together?'

A long silence followed this reasonable-sounding question. At last Marianne said, 'Toomie says it's not as simple as that.'

'Nothing is ever simple,' I sighed. 'Look, Julia, can you just tell me which way I go at this hideous junction that's coming up ahead?'

She studied the map.

'You want to take the road to Annonay.'

'There isn't one.'

'St Etienne, then. Get quickly into the outside lane.'

'Oh.'

Luckily, after an hour or so, the children, tired from our early start, fell asleep.

Whether Toomie slept or not, we could not tell. He/she never talked to us.

The hills grew steeper, the villages smaller and more scattered, the roads narrower.

At last, when we were within a mile of our destination, the children woke, yawning, stiff and thirsty.

'Are we nearly there? Oh, good!'

The last mile to Mas Honorat is all downhill. Down a single-track, narrow, precipitous, zigzag track, a dirt road which in winter becomes more of a challenge than any bobsleigh course. The view is spectacular, but passengers in cars are seldom looking at it; they are watching the distance from the wheels to the edge of the track, or praying, or keeping their eyes on their laps.

Not Toomie, though.

'Toomie says he's never, *ever*, seen anything like *this*!'

'Well, that's nice,' I said, feeling for the first time a faint warmth towards Toomie. Poor little south London brat, these French mountains must indeed be a surprise for him. Perhaps he/she had never been to the cinema. Perhaps he/she had lived before moving pictures were invented? Or photographs?

'Toomie says, what a good thing we brought the skateboard.'

'You did *what*?'

I had been aware, in a vague way, at home, that Tom, who is one of the chief skateboard stars in his playground, had said sometimes, 'Toomie loves to ride with me. They didn't have skateboards when she was alive. She thinks skateboards are really plummy.'

If we had a language expert with us, I thought, we   43

might be able to date Toomie's life in London from the use of that word plummy.

'Listen,' I said, 'I didn't know you were planning to bring the skateboard, and if I had known, I would certainly have forbidden it. Mas Honorat is no place for skateboards.'

'But why, Daddy?'

'Look at the gradient.'

Some of the zigzags were so sharp that I had to back the car down the next leg, as there was not sufficient room to make a proper turn.

'This track was made for mules, not cars or skateboards. If you went off at the corner, you'd end up at the bottom, in the fleuve, probably with a broken neck. No skateboarding.'

In fact, one of the first things I did when we arrived at the Mas, was to remove the skateboard from among Tom's T-shirts and perch it high, out of reach, on a beam in the unfinished area which would one day be the extra guest room. Mas Honorat had been constructed from the ruins of two farmhouses
on different levels of the steep hillside, and it was far

from complete. Half of each holiday we spent there was devoted to construction work.

While I was carting beams and mixing mortar and rolling rocks, Julia attended to the garden, which consisted of rockeries and tiny terraces, where grew such hardy plants as could survive deep snow in winter, roasting sun in summer, and the attentions of wandering deer and wild boar. Twice a day we took the children swimming in the river – which meant a five-mile detour down the valley and back the other side, in order to reach a spot that was exactly below Mas Honorat, only a few hundred metres down the prickly mountainside, but, from our side, inaccessible until we could afford to quarry ourselves a track down.

Toomie, it seemed, did not swim. Could not swim. Had never entered water in his/her life (even to wash? we wondered) and had no intention of starting at this stage.

After each of our swimming excursions the children were always a bit subdued for a while; it seemed that Toomie went into a sulk at being excluded from a pleasure we were all sharing.

'Though it is his own fault,' Marianne said fairly. 'I'm sure she could learn. It's silly of her to get so grumpy.'

Back at the Mas, the children and their companion occupied themselves quite peacefully for long spells of time, while Julia gardened and I carried on my building operations. On previous holidays Tom had helped, or hindered me, mixing cement and trundling wheelbarrow-loads to and fro, while Marianne played quite a useful part in Julia's garden activities. But this year they kept strictly to their own affairs.

'Well, I suppose it's quite healthy in a way,' Julia said, one evening on the terrace, as we drank wine and rested our aching backs, while the children, already in their hammocks, sleepily conversed or listened to the local radio station.

'I wonder if Toomie is picking up any French?' I said. 'And what exactly do you mean by *healthy*? Is it really healthy to play with a ghost? I do worry about what he may tell them.'

'Well, we've always said it was a pity there aren't any local children for them to play with. So I suppose 46 in a way it's as well they have Toomie.'

Ste Baume could hardly be described as a village. It was a community of scattered farms dispersed over many miles of breakneck slopes. Our nearest neighbour, Madame Berthezène, was within a hunting horn's distance as sound carried or the raven flew, but we were not ravens, and it took half an hour to reach her by car. She was an elderly widow in her late eighties, whose children, and even grandchildren, had long since predeceased her.

'Let's go and call on Madame tomorrow,' Julia said. 'I've masses of pictures for her.'

Madame collected pictures of the English royal family, and we spent our winters chopping them out of newspapers and magazines. The Queen Mother was her special favourite. 'Ah, quel courage! Quelle bonté!'

When we said we were going to call on Madame, the children, who usually adored her company, were unexpectedly reluctant.

'You'll only talk boring grown-up talk and drink horrible aniseedy drinks for hours and hours. Can't we stay at home?'

47

'Well – all right; if you'll be sensible.'

For several days past they had been absorbed in a slightly incomprehensible game involving the use of a number of sawn-off rounds of tree trunk, fuel for the stove, which they used as stools, or stepping-stones, or building material. '*Don't* move that, please, it's Toomie's palace wall!'

'Oh, sorry. Must he have his palace right in front of the kitchen door?'

'It's the only flat place.'

Well, that was true. But, otherwise, it seemed a harmless occupation.

Only once had I been obliged to issue a veto, when they began rolling the rounds of wood down the mountainside.

'Please stop that, it's dangerous.'

'Why?'

'Well, firstly there's a bit of cliff below the house, you can't see who might be down at the bottom. People come there to fish. And no one wants a ten-pound log falling on his head. And, secondly, it took a lot of trouble carting these logs here. We don't want them wasted.'

Tom took this prohibition in good part.

'Actually,' he said, 'it was Toomie's idea.'

Toomie, apparently, went into another of her sulks.

'Toomie and Tom like playing boys' games,' Marianne later confided gloomily to Julia. 'It's not much fun for me with them any more. I'd rather help you with the garden.'

'Well, when we come back from Madame's, you and I can plant a row of lettuce seedlings. She says she's got some to give me.'

'Can I come with you?' said Marianne unexpectedly. 'To Madame? I'd like to see her.'

'And leave Tom on his own? No, I don't think that would be such a good plan.'

'He'd have Toomie.'

'A ghost isn't really enough company,' said Julia.

In the car, on the way to Madame's house, she said, 'And I'm beginning to think that Toomie isn't a good influence. I'm a bit anxious about what she tells them.'

'I've thought that all along.'

'I wish we could think of some way of getting rid of him.'

'Me too,' I said with feeling.

'But I don't suppose there's any chance of its happening in France. Perhaps when we get back to Camberwell . . .'

Madame was desolated not to see les petites anges. 'I have been baking some special cakes for them. Well, you must take them when you go. But please, please bring Tom and Marianne to visit me very soon. Onyx is sad not to see them, also.'

Onyx was her immense, blunt-faced brown mountain dog, reputed to have rescued several snow-bound travellers in the course of his long life.

We spent a pleasant hour with Madame, who was a kindly, massive lady, exuding bounty. But then she grew unexpectedly fidgety.

'No, I don't like it too much that you leave those children on their own. It is better you should return to them.'

In fact we had been feeling the same way, and
50 left her terrace readily enough. Mas Honorat was

not visible from her ridge of the mountain.

'As a matter of fact, Madame, they aren't entirely alone,' Julia explained, to give the conversation a more cheerful turn, for Madame's brow was furrowed with worry. 'They have their ghost friend with them.'

'Hein? Un revenant?'

Explanations about Toomie took quite a little while, during which I was dying to get away. To my surprise, Madame received Julia's account with total seriousness.

'For myself, I have a complete belief in phantoms,' she said. 'I am a sensitive, you see, un medium, how do you say it in English?'

'A medium. Same word.'

'After people die, sometimes it happens that the spirit lingers for a while, confused, lonely, uncomprehending. Then it longs for company. So that is why, doubtless, this sad little ghost has attached itself to your pair. But it is not a desirable relationship.'

'No, *that* it isn't,' I agreed. 'But why do you think so, Madame?'

'Because it will be most natural that this ghostly *copain* may wish that one of the children, or both, 51 should also become a spirit. So as to ensure permanent companionship. Whereas, of course, this Toomie should be working to free himself from all the ties that still attach him to this world and his former life. And travelling on to greater freedom.'

'Yes, I see. And I quite agree.'

'I wish you will go home *now,* at once,' said Madame forcefully.

I drove as fast as I could; but you really cannot hurry on those tracks.

At the top of the drive down to Mas Honorat we met Marianne, looking tearful and distressed. She hurled herself into the car.

'I was coming to get you! Toomie has talked Tom into getting down the skateboard.'

'But how could he possibly? How could they reach it?'

The ladder, I had taken care, hung high enough so that Tom, on his own, could not get it down.

'Oh, they are piling up those bits of log to make a staircase. And then they are going to ride down The Slope. *Please* hurry, Daddy.'

She was on Julia's lap, and I was feather-stitching my way down the zigzag with infinite, frantic, desperate care.

The Slope was what we called the forty-five degree angle of mountainside that connected all the zigs and zags of the track. A long, lethal slant of it lay above and on the far side of the house. I did not dare look in that direction, as I guided the car down on to its usual stopping place, but Julia suddenly said, 'I can see them,' in a voice so dry and faint that it sounded as if her throat were full of sand.

I leapt out of the car and shouted, '*Tom!* Stop that!'

'*Tom!*' screamed Marianne. 'Toomie wants to *hurt* you!' Julia had raced into the house. I could not think what for, until I saw her reappear, dragging the enormous beanbag which served us as a sofa on wet days.

'You brilliant woman!' I croaked, in a voice as dry as hers, and helped her shove and haul it up the dusty slope, and place it in the track of the oncoming Tom.

'*Wheeee!*' he was shouting. 'Isn't this *plummy!* Hey, Toomie! We must be going a hundred miles an hour!' 53

The beanbag stopped them. Stopped Tom, and the skateboard, at all events.

Tom was considerably cut and grazed. But what really shook him was our passion, and our rage against Toomie.

'He didn't mean any harm. *Honestly,* Daddy. It was just a game.'

'You are not to play with Toomie *any* more. At all. *Ever.* And I am going to chop up the skateboard and burn it.'

Tom went weeping off to his hammock.

The atmosphere at Mas Honorat was dreadful.

'Toomie's terribly upset,' Marianne told us. 'And angry, too. He doesn't understand at all why you are so cross. And, actually, I don't see how you *can* stop Tom playing with her.'

Nor did we.

'I'm going to go and see Madame,' said Julia.

While she was gone, I carried out my threat, chopping the skateboard into firewood, removing its wheels, and stuffing it into the stove. While I per-
54 formed these actions I felt surrounded by cold, malig-

nant silence. It took no effort at all to imagine Toomie at my elbow, watching, speechless, furious, waiting his chance to do me a bad turn.

When Julia returned, Madame followed behind in her own car.

'In our hurry we forgot Madame's delicious cakes,' Julia said, and took them into the children's room. A silence lingered behind her as she emerged; I hoped very much that it came from contented nibbling.

Madame sat upright in our wooden armchair. Onyx, who had accompanied her, placed himself with gravity, equally upright, beside her.

'Tell me again what happened,' said Madame, and listened, nodding, to our account.

'It may well be, as Tom says, that the little revenant meant no *harm,* in our sense of the word, to Tom,' she then pronounced. 'After all, to him, death is no different from life . . . Eh, mon Dieu! Regardez Onyx!'

The monumental and dignified Onyx was lying on his back, waving paws in the air, an expression of idiotic bliss on his face.

'Toomie is rubbing his stomach,' explained Marianne, who had come quietly from the children's room. And she added, in a low voice, 'I believe Toomie thinks that Onyx is Chap.'

'And who was Chap?' inquired Madame.

'Chap was Toomie's dog.'

Madame nodded. 'Who knows, maybe it was so? Who knows if dogs have souls too, and can come back? Maybe those two arranged, long ago, to meet here?'

She addressed the air.

'Toomie? Ecoute, mon enfant! You are now coming home to live with me, and Onyx. Comprends-tu?'

'Can you *see* Toomie, Madame?' whispered Marianne, awestruck.

'Almost,' said Madame Berthezène, with her severe smile.

I knew what she meant. I myself had *almost* seen Toomie sitting on Tom's shoulders, atop of the skateboard.

Madame got up and left, Onyx following. We
56 heard the sound of her car start and drive off.

Marianne went into the children's room and said, 'Tom: Toomie has gone to live with Madame and Onyx.'

A very long silence followed. Then Tom muttered, in a choked, tearful voice, 'Well, perhaps it's a good thing. Madame always said she was sorry not to have children in her house. And we can always go and see Toomie when we come for the holidays.'

I suppose that is true, I thought, with little enthusiasm.

But a cold, early autumn set in that year, after we had left Ste Baume at the end of August, and a ferocious, freezing winter. Blizzards and avalanches were frequent. One of the avalanches swept down the mountainside and removed Madame's house, with her inside it, Onyx, her furniture, and all her pictures of the British royal family.

'Perhaps she and Toomie and Onyx are all keeping each other company somewhere,' Tom said sadly, when we received this news.

But I hoped that Madame, and Toomie also, had travelled on to a greater freedom. As she herself would have put it.

PENGUIN CHILDREN'S 60s

ALI BABA AND THE FORTY THIEVES • *Retold by N. J. Dawood*

THE AMAZING PIPPI LONGSTOCKING • *Astrid Lindgren*

ANNE AT GREEN GABLES • *L. M. Montgomery*

AT THE RIVER-GATES AND
OTHER SUPERNATURAL STORIES • *Philippa Pearce*

CLASSIC GHOST STORIES

CLASSIC NONSENSE VERSE

THE CLOCKWORK MOUSE • *Dick King-Smith*

DEAD MAN'S LANE • *Joan Aiken*

THE DRAGON ON THE ROOF • *Terry Jones*

FOUR GREAT GREEK MYTHS • *Roger Lancelyn Green*

THE GREAT MOUSE PLOT AND
OTHER TALES OF CHILDHOOD • *Roald Dahl*

THE GREAT TIME WARP ADVENTURE • *Jon Scieszka*

THE HOOLIGAN'S SHAMPOO • *Philip Ridley*

KEEP IT IN THE FAMILY • *Anne Fine*

KING ARTHUR'S COURT • *Roger Lancelyn Green*

THE LITTLE MERMAID AND
OTHER FAIRY TALES • *Hans Andersen (Translated by Naomi Lewis)*

LOST DOG AND OTHER STORIES • *Penelope Lively*

THE MIDNIGHT STORY • *Margaret Mahy*

MOOMINTROLLS AND FRIENDS • *Tove Jansson*

MRS PEPPERPOT TURNS DETECTIVE • *Alf Prøysen*

THE NIGHT TRAIN: STORIES IN PROSE AND VERSE • *Allan Ahlberg*

THE PIED PIPER OF HAMELIN AND OTHER CLASSIC STORIES IN VERSE

ROBIN HOOD AND HIS MERRY MEN • *Roger Lancelyn Green*

SHERLOCK HOLMES AND THE SPECKLED BAND • *Sir Arthur Conan Doyle*

SMACKING MY LIPS • *Michael Rosen*

TALES FROM ALICE IN WONDERLAND • *Lewis Carroll*

TALES FROM THE JUNGLE BOOK • *Rudyard Kipling*

THREE QUIRKY TAILS • *Paul Jennings*

TOM SAWYER'S PIRATE ADVENTURE • *Mark Twain*

TOM THUMB AND OTHER FAIRY TALES • *Jacob and Wilhelm Grimm*